More of
Grandfather's Stories From Mexico

Written by Donna Roland
Illustrations by Ron Oden

Adapted from the Mexican Folktale
"Salvador and Señor Coyote"

Meet Carlos and Maria.

Carlos and Maria live in America with their mother and father and their baby sister.

Carlos and Maria have a grandfather who lives in Mexico and often comes to visit them. When grandfather comes to visit, he tells Carlos and Maria stories about Mexico.

They're stories that Carlos and Maria
love to hear over and over. One of their
favorite stories is the story about
Salvador the burro.

Salvador lived on a ranch, which was called a hacienda. He loved living on the hacienda. Many other burros lived there, too.

Every day Miguel would feed the burros
and put packs on their backs and go
into town. Salvador loved going to
town, even though the load on his
back was sometimes heavy. He was
proud to be so strong.

When they came back from town,
Miguel would give everyone corn and
green grass to eat. Then they would
rest, listening to the music and singing
of the people.

On Sunday everyone rested. All the
burros would go to the mountain and
eat the green grass. Salvador stayed
near the others so he could always see
the Oldest Burro, who was very wise.

One Sunday Salvador found a place
where the grass was very sweet. He got
so excited that he forgot to watch the
others. He ate and ate, never looking
up.

All at once the green grass ended and there was a stream. Salvador put his nose in and took a drink. Then he raised his head and looked around. He was all alone.

There were no other burros, but he could hear someone laughing. Then he saw an animal that looked like a dog standing on the other side of the stream.

"You must be hungry. You have been eating like a pig," said the strange animal. "Oh, no. Pigs eat the roots; I only eat the tops," answered Salvador. The strange animal only laughed.

"My name is Salvador. I am a burro, and I live at the big hacienda," said the little burro. "I know that," said the stranger. "I am Raul the coyote."

"I am the wisest of all the animals in the woods." "Oh," said Salvador. "It must be nice to be so wise and know so much. I am not as lucky."

The two talked for quite a while. The
coyote told the little burro he must be
dumb to carry things on his back and
never to have been in the woods
before.

Raul talked about many wonderful
things. He asked Salvador if he would
like to come with him. He would show
the world to him, and all the things he
had been missing out on.

Just then the little burro heard the Oldest Burro calling him and he ran back to the others. All week long he thought about what wonderful things Raul had talked about.

When Sunday came again, Salvador went back to the same place, hoping to find the coyote. He waited. Raul finally came. "If you are coming with me," he said, "we must leave now."

Salvador did not want to miss out on anything, so the two of them crossed the stream and headed toward the woods. It wasn't easy for Salvador to keep up with Raul, since Raul didn't stay on any path.

Raul also went under many low branches. As it began to get dark, it was hard for Salvador to see where he was going. The little burro wanted to stop and rest.

Raul told him they couldn't stop–there were hunters out, and until they were deep in the woods they were not safe. For the first time Salvador was afraid, even though he didn't know what hunters were.

At last they stopped. Salvador was
more tired than he had even been
before. "Well, here we are," said the
coyote. "Now let's go get something
to eat." "Can we sleep first?" asked the
little burro.

Raul told Salvador it would soon be morning, and it would be too light to hunt. Salvador thought that was strange. Everyone he knew could see better when it was light. "I sleep when the sun goes down, not when it comes up," cried the little burro.

"I miss eating corn and having a warm bed of straw to lie in. I don't sleep in a hole! I want to go back to the hacienda. That's where I belong."

He headed home, to the hacienda
where Miguel had corn and green
grass waiting for him, where all
Salvador had to do was be a burro.
And that's what he enjoyed being the
most.